The MOMologues

The original comedy about
motherhood

by Lisa Rafferty,
Stefanie Cloutier and
Sheila Eppolito

A SAMUEL FRENCH ACTING EDITION

SAMUEL FRENCH

FOUNDED 1830

NEW YORK HOLLYWOOD LONDON TORONTO

SAMUELFRENCH.COM

ISBN 978-0-573-69739-5   Printed in U.S.A.   #29182

MUSIC USE NOTE

IMPORTANT BILLING AND CREDIT REQUIREMENTS

The MOMologues was originally presented at the ICA Theatre in Boston on May 3, 2002. It was directed by Lisa Rafferty, with lighting by Heidi Hinkel, and costumes by Kim Dickinson. The production stage manager was Kristie Froman. The original cast was Stefanie Cloutier, Charlotte Dietz, Ellen Stone and Maria Wardwell.

The MOMologues returned to the ICA Theatre in Boston on April 23, 2003. Again, it was directed by Lisa Rafferty, with lighting by Heidi Hinkel, and costumes by Kim Dickinson. The stage manager was Kristie Froman. The four original cast members returned – Stefanie Cloutier, Charlotte Dietz, Ellen Stone and Maria Wardwell – with three of the cast members "job sharing" the roles with Jane Eyler, Johanna Perri and Cinda Donovan, respectively.

In April 2004, *The MOMologues* opened in Boston's theater district at the Stuart Street Playhouse, Second Stage. It was directed by Lisa Rafferty, lighting by Ken Elliot, costumes by Kimmerie Jones, and stage managed by Hadley Tieger. It was produced by Rita Fucillo and Lisa Rafferty and the company manager was David Polanzak. The show featured a rotating cast of 11 actors who shared the four roles including: Jennifer Burke, Stefanie Cloutier, Charlotte Dietz, Cinda Donovan, Lisa Caron Driscoll, Jane Eyler, Johanna Perri, Lea Renay, Ellen Stone, Holly Vanasse and Maria Wardwell.

At the same time, the show traveled to the Palace Theater in Manchester, New Hampshire for a show on April 23, 2004; the Company Theater in Norwell, Massachusetts for three shows on May 7, 8 and 9, 2004; and the Regent Theatre in Arlington, Massachusetts for a show on June 5, 2004. Various members of the Boston cast appeared at those theatres.

CHARACTERS

Charlotte
Ellen
Maria
Stefanie

SETTING

One chair with a small table with phone down left, one chair with a small table down right. Up left is a round table with two chairs and up right is a park bench.

ACT I

(Suggested preshow music: Mother-themed songs like Supremes "Baby Love," Beatles "Lady Madonna," Paul Simon's "Mother and Child Reunion," "Mother's Little Helper" by the Rolling Stones, etc.*)

(Lights up on **THREE WOMEN** *dressed in career clothes, carrying briefcases.)*

STEF. I spent my twenties trying not to get pregnant, and my thirties trying desperately to get pregnant.

MARIA. We were lucky – it happened right away – wow, I'm pregnant!…NOW WHAT???

CHAR. Clomid, Pergonal, luteal phase, cervical mucus, basal body temperature, ovulation, insemination – who knew trying to have a baby would be so scientific?

*(***WOMEN*** exit as* **ELLEN** *walks in:)*

ELLEN. After the old fashioned way didn't work, my husband and I went in to learn all about the administering of fertility drugs. The popular drug at the time – Pergonal – came from the urine of post-menopausal Italian nuns, I kid you not…It is meant to be injected into your hip with a hypodermic syringe the size of a screwdriver. I am clinically averse to any kind of needle – after all, I had been lying to doctors for years about having a tetanus shot…So the nurse suggests my husband practice on an orange first, and then announces he's ready to go. Here? Now? OOOOOKAAAAY. I lean forward on to the examining table, hold my breath, and just as he's about to jab me, the nurse says – "Don't hold back now – just pretend you are playing darts and she's the bullseye – now go…"

(**ELLEN** *exits,* **MARIA** *walks on:*)

MARIA. OK – so my husband and I decide we are ready to try and have a baby – so I look up "how to get pregnant" in this crunchy-granola book. I read the bar graph that pinpoints the approximate time of the month that ovulation occurs. I open up my day planner and look at the date. I look at the bar graph in the book. I stare at my day planner. I walk over to my husband and say: um – ya know, according to this book, tonight would be, you know – the night. He says: "Great – let's go!" That was it. Boom. One try. Mission accomplished.

(over to:)

CHAR. For me, deciding to get pregnant and getting pregnant were two totally different things. For years I had faithfully used birth control but after six months of no-holds-barred, unprotected sex, and still no sign of sperm meeting egg, I began the circuit of fertility testing and basal body temp charting. Now, the basal body temp thing was pretty interesting [insert digital thermometer into mouth], take your temperature at the same time every morning, before you've so much as moved a muscle, never mind going to the bathroom, and at some point you'll see a spike in your temperature, which tells you the egg has dropped. Of course, the secret is to have the sperm in place BEFORE the egg drops, so the timing of sex became pretty tricky. And with all this charting and testing going on, sex wasn't exactly about sex anymore, it was more like a job you had to get up and go to whether you wanted to or not. Most of the time, there was nothing I wanted to do LESS than have sex. And then, finally, after months of charting and testing and completely scheduled sex, the stars aligned, one of his sperm made it to the egg! Hallelujah! At last we could stop with the fucking sex! Funny thing though, the more pregnant I got, the hornier I became. Something to do with hormones and blood flow to the vagina, but there I was, hugely pregnant, with no easy way to PERFORM the act, begging my husband to give it a try. I was THAT horny....When the o.b. came in shortly after I'd pushed out my nine pound daughter and told me "No sex for six weeks," I thought, you silly, silly man, it'll be SIX YEARS before I let my husband near me again!

(**CHAR** *exits.* **STEFANIE** *enters on the phone:*)

STEF. Mum? It's me. I saw it today! The baby! We had an ultrasound, and saw the little heart beating. There wasn't much to see – it looked like a bowl of hot & sour soup actually, but when we saw the little heart kind of light up with each beat the relief was wonderful... What? Me too. I feel like this one's going to hang in and be fine. Anyhow...Yes. I feel good too, Mum. This one's going to happen.

(*next in:*)

ELLEN. OK – let's get a couple of things straight... First, morning sickness is a misnomer. Verge-of-barfing-all-day-and-night-sickness is more accurate. And the glow of pregnancy? Hides the unglamorous reality – the bloating, swelling, indigestion, heartburn, hemorrhoids, fatigue...yuck! From your very first o.b. appointment, your dignity pretty much goes out the window. But there's nothing in the world that compares to those anxious moments when your doctor is moving that instrument over your belly trying to find the first heartbeat. And then wow! – when you hear it – it sounds like a "swish swish" in your own private seashore...and you literally feel your heart swell with a rush of some primordial motherhood hormone. Then you start to show and actually look pregnant, which sure beats just looking chubby and the onslaught of unsolicited advice begins, and never ends... And, you just cannot believe how much nerve total strangers have in telling you peculiar, private, sometimes horrifying things – and the hands-on contact! Private personal space has no meaning when your belly sticks out from here to Sunday. Everyone seems fascinated... If you're the kind of person who likes attention, you'll love being pregnant...

*(ELLEN picks up her bag as **CHARLOTTE, STEF** and **MARIA** surround her.)*

STEF. Wow – you're huge – how far along are you?

MARIA. Did you plan this pregnancy?

CHAR. My gawd – you're so big – do you really have four months to go?

STEF. I drank and smoked through all my pregnancies and my kids turned out all right.

CHAR. You're not supposed to drink wine or anything – ever, not a teeny bit, not for any reason. Don't even think about it.

MARIA. I just had a miscarriage – you know one out of four pregnancies end that way.

CHAR. Bagels, pizza, junk food – no, no, no. All empty calories you know…

MARIA. You're going to nurse that baby aren't you?

STEF. You really need to nurse for a full year.

CHAR. You really should nurse for two years.

MARIA. You can mix a bottle with nursing at the beginning, don't let anyone tell you that you can't.

STEF. Whatever you do, don't mix breast and bottle.

CHAR. Are you finding out what you're having?

MARIA. You're carrying way in front – it must be a boy.

STEF. Gaining weight in your face means you are having a girl…

CHAR. Are you hoping for a boy?

MARIA. Girl?

STEF. You're not going back to work are you?

CHAR. Is this your first?

STEF. Don't be a martyr, honey, take the drugs. *(walks out of scene discreetly)*

MARIA. I really think women should give birth the natural way.

CHAR. If it's a boy, he shouldn't be circumcised you know.

MARIA. If it's a boy, you're going to have him circumcised right?

CHAR. Your life is about to change forever...

MARIA. Your life will never be the same...

C&M. It's the toughest job you'll ever love!

(STEF in:)

STEF. *(on phone)*: Mum? Oh, thank God you're there. I think I'm getting to the scary part of pregnancy... my ass is falling out. Really and truly, parts of my ass have left my body...I know they're hemorrhoids. Tuck them in?...WHAT? Wear gloves and tuck them back in? Jesus. Another closely guarded secret discovered... Why doesn't anybody ever tell you this shit? Yup... Thanks, Mum...

(Lights up on CHARLOTTE and ELLEN [both quite pregnant] at a Starbucks table up left:)

CHAR. Nothing like an extra decaf venti mocha frappucino to get you through the day...

ELLEN. Yeah, I'm pretty tired of this pregnancy diet restriction thing. I mean, avoiding alcohol and caffeine is one thing...

CHAR. ...but it's like no wine, no diet Snapple...

ELLEN. ...nothing sweet, nothing fattening, and drink lots and lots of milk. And just be healthy as you can be dammit.

CHAR. And I'm gaining more weight than I ever thought possible. I've always had a high and low weight number in my head. The dream weight, that I'll never be again and the nightmare weight number that as I approach I head straight for Jenny Craig. Well, I knew it was going to be trouble when at my second appointment I already exceeded the nightmare weight number by five pounds.

ELLEN. It's pretty friggin' bad news when you step on the doctor's scale and they have to move the big bottom weight over to 150...scary!

CHAR. And what's up with checking your weight first and then checking your blood pressure? I mean, what the hell do they think my blood pressure is going to be after I get weighed?

ELLEN. I always starve myself the morning of the appointment, as if not eating those few hours will make a big difference. And it goes without saying that I take my shoes off before getting on that scale...

CHAR. Of course...and how about the sex thing? Kind've weird in this condition don't you think?

ELLEN. My cousin Debbie told me that she was really horny through most of her pregnancy, just couldn't get enough. She thought maybe it was the way the baby sat inside. Whatever it was, I could use a little of it. I have nothing. It's as if all my sex hormones detoured right through the umbilical cord and into producing the baby. It isn't that sex is unpleasant, it just feels like a trip through a Jiffy Lube. Charity sex is what it comes down to, my poor husband. And now that we are nearing the end, when I am blown up like a hydroblimp, we have some...ahhh, access challenges. Sort of like finding your way onto the Leverett Circle onramp *(or some other local geographic reference...)*

CHAR. Oh my god...

ELLEN. Ah well – it won't be long now, and then, from what I understand, the real fun begins...

(ELLEN and CHARLOTTE exit. A very pregnant MARIA walks on.)

MARIA. Balsamic vinegar. Thai food. A long walk through a Japanese Garden. Nipple stimulation. Or the lady who took one look at me as I waddled around the mall and said, "Honey, you need to go home and do the nasty with your husband..." These things are supposed to start you in labor as you head down the home stretch. When you are SO READY to have the baby. When that baby is like a guest who has stayed too long...And all the phone calls from people who can't BELIEVE you haven't had the baby yet. And the weekly – or daily – doctor's appointments. It's like the whole world is focused on your cervix. The waiting, the wondering. Was that a Braxton Hicks or the real thing? It sure feels real. But I could still talk while it was happening. They told me I wouldn't be able to talk. Why does my back hurt? Why am I cleaning everything in sight? Am I nesting? Am I a bird for christ sake? Where is the baby? I'm done, over done, well done. Done, done, done!

(**ELLEN** *and* **CHARLOTTE** *– now postpartum – on three chairs down center.*)

ELLEN. So about those Lamaze classes…

CHAR. My labor was certainly NOT how they describe it in Lamaze classes…

ELLEN. Did you think they helped at all?

CHAR. Fucking useless. I mean, REALLY.

(**MARIA** *joins them with chair after having changed out of her pregnancy pillow.*)

ELLEN. Yeah, I like the advice about all the walking, massaging and relaxing stuff that should happen at the hospital before the baby is born. I mean, I actually brought a tennis ball with me so my husband could rub my back. But, you know, my water broke at home and WHAM – hard contractions a minute apart, I got thrown in a bed with every medical contraption they could round up – then I screamed bloody murder for seven hours till I got an epidural…

CHAR. With my first, I labored, or so I thought, all day. I sashayed into the hospital, told them I was there to have a baby – and the nurse looks me up and down and says "Honey, you look WAY too happy to be here. You can tell your husband not to pay the parking, 'cause you are going RIGHT home."

MARIA. I finally went into labor while I was at work, in the middle of the city. The company nurse insists on putting me in a wheelchair to take me out through the lobby – during lunch hour. She wheeled me outside – through sidewalk construction – when we hit a bump and I go flying into traffic...

ELLEN. That night, when I went into labor, just as my husband and I got home very late from a Christmas party, and we were in bed, exhausted, when I looked at him and said, "Well, either the baby just kicked me in the bladder or my water just broke." And he turned to me and said: "Well, I hope it's your bladder because I'm too tired to have a baby tonight."

CHAR. With my twins, I popped the first one out and he was literally caught by a one-gloved o.b. – the labor nurse started screaming at me to "close my legs" and stop pushing. Stop pushing? Fuck that!

MARIA. So what was your favorite part of labor and delivery?

CHAR. Gosh, there's so much to choose from, I just couldn't say. Maybe it was the hours of literally feeling that my body was splitting in two...

ELLEN. Ooh, I know, it was answering the litany of authorized hospital questions from the nurse as I was on the bed, groaning in agony...social security number? 183-79- aagh! No, no allergies, HUT HUT HOOoooo. Primary physician? Are you NUTS? ASK MY HUSBAND – DOES HE LOOK BUSY?!

MAR. Well, when I was laying there, pushing for all I'm worth and the doctor says, "So, how do you feel about episiotomies?" And I'm thinking, gee, I love it when someone cuts through a muscle in a very sensitive place on my body. And she says, "It's better than tearing down there," which is exactly what I'm thinking. She takes a very sharp pair of scissors and points them in a place I'd rather not think about. And later, when she's stitching and stitching down there, I tell her "You know, some of those holes are SUPPOSED to be there!"

ELLEN. I actually asked for a couple of EXTRA stitches… my fear was that after the baby came through I'd be as big as the Callahan tunnel. *(or local reference)*

CHAR. And afterwards, wasn't it just a little weird to feel that scar? I mean, I guess I knew WHERE they were cutting, but I just didn't really think about it until weeks later, in the shower, when I thought, My GOD, that scar heads right up into me!

MAR. Ah, the joy of delivering your little miracle into the world…

> *(**CHARLOTTE** and **ELLEN** exit, **MARIA** acts as "nurse" helping **STEF** sit down left, with her feet on a chair and handing her the phone – then exits:)*

STEF. Mum? It's me. How was the wedding? I can't believe you guys were all at the wedding and I missed it. I sort of remember talking to you last night, but I probably wasn't making much sense. Did I tell you I decided on her name? Sophie…Yup. Oh my gawd, it was so scary, you know? They broke my water, and we're off to the races, right? Then the nurse puts the fetal monitor back on and there wasn't ANYTHING. I'm watching her face, and as good as she is, I can see she's worried. So she hits some button behind me, and a flood of people come flying in, and meanwhile the nurse has her hand inside me, but I don't care, because I can see things are going south fast. The nurse says "cord is prolapsed," and someone unhitches my bed from the wall, and I'm whisked down the hall. So the pictures start in my head, zooming and ugly, of us as parents with this baby in a wheelchair and me forever changed…So I start to pray, to Mary, because I figure she's a mother too, right? So I do the Hail Mary like an auctioneer, with my eyes closed because I can't stand to see the gray faces everywhere…We're running now, to an operating room, and my body is out there for all to see with some stranger's hand up inside me, and then the anesthesia guy says that this is the fast acting stuff, and if I just count back from 100 and a mask goes over my face and I pass out... And that's it, eleven minutes from start to finish. From the water breaking to the baby's birth – eleven minutes.... What?... Yes, she's beautiful. She's got a perfect c-section head, not all traumatized from regular delivery, But I'm still a little freaked out. I'm still in the middle of what-almost-was. I know she's fine, Mom, I do. And I just about got a callous from pushing the lousy morphine beeper. It's set to give you a dose every seven minutes...RIGHT! Seven minutes! I asked the nurse, "What happens if I hit the beeper more than once every seven minutes?" And she says, "Nothing," except they keep a log of your beeps. So now they think I'm Janice Joplin or something...

(Brief fade – not to black – then lights back up again:)

STEF. *(cont.)* Mum? It's me. She's so sweet it's staggering. Today I laid down next to her on my bed while she napped, and I smelled her head, and thanked God for the millionth time that she's perfect. And then I stuck my face right next to hers and breathed her in; I mean I took in what she breathed out. I just wanted to have her in me again, even for a minute...I won't let anybody visit – I think everyone thinks I'm a little whacked – but I'm just being with her. Yeah, the pain is better too...The doctor gave me some opium knock-off and it doesn't hurt so much. And I held her, and I cried for a long time for all of it, and I think I've forgiven her. And so now we're starting over.

*(Fade out a little then **MARIA** walks in with her planner, **CHARLOTTE** enters with a "What to Expect" book – on bench – and **ELLEN** with photos and photo album to work on – at the table:)*

MARIA. I've loved my day planner since the first day I was introduced to it, at a work seminar. I used it every day: it had my daily task list, appointments, important conversations, voicemail records – everything. I lived by this book. When I got pregnant, I even marked the baby's due date in it, in big bold letters. After I had my baby, I kept using it for all my new mom information – I'd mark when the baby ate and which breast I started on, how many times the baby pooped and peed and who gave what gift. And when I go back to work, I'll use it for all my work stuff and playdates and gymboree lessons. I love my planner. I don't know how people organize their children without one! (**MARIA** *exits.*)

CHAR. I always figured I'd have children some day. Doesn't every little girl have a baby doll that she loves to dress and undress and push around in anything resembling a doll carriage? Anyway, I was never very clear on the details, just knew that I'd have children one day…So, I graduated from college and spent my twenties building my career, meeting guys, partying with friends, and the marriage thing happens in my thirties. Then MORE years traveling with my husband, cementing my career, and we finally got around to having kids. So, after much trying and testing, we finally had our first baby. Our little bundle of joy. Or so baby commercials and magazines would have you believe – you know the shots of sweet little crawling, gurgling, dimply babies…I can't believe I was sucked in so easily. After being discharged from the hospital, the visiting nurse showed up to check on us and as soon as I saw her, I burst into tears. The baby had been crying nonstop for the past three hours, my milk hadn't yet come in, and I was exhausted from walking endless laps around the dining room, rocking and cooing and singing to this tiny torturer. And that was just day three of motherhood… (**CHARLOTTE** *exits.*)

ELLEN. Time does strange things once you have a baby in your arms. Everyone says things to you like "cherish your time with them – they will be grown up before you know it…" And on the one hand, you are in awe of the new miracle in your life. Time seems to stand still when you are marveling at all they do and how they look. That's the wonderful part... But time slows down in another way – I mean damn near stops... Like on those nights when your new baby is crying relentlessly and you are desperate for sleep, or when the "arsenic hour" begins in the evening with the requisite irritability and inconsolable hysteria. Then time creeps forward in some warped parents-only mode. Instead of dog years, they should have something called mommy minutes... Like the minutes after you have finally gotten your newborn to sleep at three a.m., but you want to wait just a little longer to make sure he won't scream again when you put him down... I used to count to one hundred slowly – and then count by five's to make sure, and then count backwards from one hundred just to make doubly sure and then put my son down. Then I would stagger to bed to catch two hours sleep, and of course that would fly by in a millisecond....

(**MARIA** *and* **CHARLOTTE** *on the bench.*)

MARIA. I've always knew that I would breastfeed – I don't know, it just seemed like it would be great the closeness, the bonding...It just seemed practical...

CHAR. Really!? I really thought the whole thing was kind've...well, gross really, but felt I had to give it a try. Every two hours hooking up and wincing in pain through the whole thing. Yeah, loving that vampire-like suction on my bleeding nipples. There was no bonding, let me tell you, only resentment.

MARIA. I don't know, it was the easiest thing in the world for me, especially when I was home on my maternity leave. It was great that I could just sit and feed him and not have to think about anything.

CHAR. Not think about it! Damn, I was obsessed with just getting though five minutes of the torture – okay I'm supposed to hang in there for two weeks – uh huh, like anyone would voluntarily sit through a root canal for two weeks...No thank YOU. Nudge my husband at two a.m. to get the bottle, and I am feeling much more love for that newborn.

MARIA. Yeah, but for me it was just open my pajamas and it's there – the right amount, the right temperature. I could sleep through the whole thing.

CHAR. You're lucky. I mean the bottle thing is a pain – the sterilized water – the cost of it – it's like liquid gold... But my mom can give the bottle, a babysitter, anyone...

MARIA. Yeah, well, I just pump a lot when I want someone else to feed him. But there are downsides, I mean it's not always easy to find a place to open my blouse, whipping it out in public. Have you ever tried to find a place to nurse in a mall? I finally did it in the food court; I figured everyone else was eating there, why not him?

CHAR. Well, maybe when I have another, it will go easier, but believe me, the best bonding I ever did with my daughter was when I wasn't in agony trying to feed her!

MARIA. Oh, I plan to nurse until he's ready to give it up. A lot of the books say it's great to continue nursing, you know, for the comfort and bonding, until the child is really ready.

CHAR. So you mean you would actually keep nursing him at TWO years old?!

MARIA. Uh-huh. I have one friend whose daughter is three and still likes to nurse in the morning and at bedtime; it helps to calm her.

CHAR. Yeah, better save your money for THAT therapy later! I can't imagine my walking, talking toddler lifting up my shirt when she needs comfort!

(They get up to leave.)

MARIA. Hey, in other countries women breastfeed their children till three or four, and they all grow up ok.

CHAR. Those are also countries where breasts aren't sex objects...

MARIA. Is that good or bad?

CHAR. Oh honey, that's a bad thing...

(They exit.)

(over to:)

STEF. Mum?…Help! My milk has come in, and my breasts are on fire. Huge, fiery volcanoes of searing molten lava. Yup! I've got the ice packs on them.… I'm not even going to nurse the baby for christ sake and I've got milk here for a small third world country. Got milk? the ad says. Ya, I got milk. I got milk into my armpits, I'm serious. Mum, please tell me how you did this five times!

(next is:)

MARIA. So I go back to work after my son is born, and I'm still breastfeeding. Which means of course, pumping milk, which means pumping at work. So every day, at the appointed time according to my day planner, I would close the door of my office, pull out my semi-discreet little electronic La Leche pump thing and go at it, so to speak. All I could think about was everyone in the office standing outside my door, listening to the hum of the breast pump, wondering, "What the hell is she doing in there anyway? Is that a vibrator?" I was horrified to think of anyone finding out that I was sitting in my office half naked during my lunch hour – even though I was providing nourishment for my four month-old son. So, I concealed all evidence and prayed I wouldn't start leaking during a meeting, I kept this up for five more months until my mother made me listen to reason. The bottle worked great and I learned much later on, no one in my office ever had a clue what I was doing all that time…

*(**MARIA** is joined by **CHARLOTTE** and **STEF.** at the bench.)*

CHAR. What do you miss most?

MARIA. What do you mean?

CHAR. If your life is divided into before kids, and after kids - what do you miss most?

STEF. Privacy … alone time … solitude … I want one day - just one day, where I get up in the morning and I say to myself - "I wonder what I should do today??"

MARIA. Yeah, small, tiny amounts of time become crucial in getting through the day – or the week. Ten wonderful minutes of peace - or being in the shower without worrying about the health and safety of my baby! A short lunch break at work ...

CHAR. ... Remember reading?

MARIA & STEF. Reading?

CHAR. You know ... real life, grown up, *New York Times* Bestseller list reading ....

MARIA. You mean books with words and no pictures?

STEF. Books that use complex literary devices such as irony, metaphor, three dimensional characters - by Tolstoy, Steinbeck and Danielle Steele?

CHAR. Exactly. I'm not talking about..."Miss Lucy called the doctor, Miss Lucy called the nurse..."

MARIA & STEF. Miss Lucy called the lady with the alligator purse!"

MARIA. "Once upon a time there lived..."

CHAR. " ...three little pigs..."

STEF. "...three little bears ...'

MARIA. '... three little kittens...'

CHAR. '... a beautiful princess and a handsome prince!' Blech.

MARIA. 'Hey diddle diddle!'

CHAR. Excuse me?

STEF. 'The cat and the fiddle'

CHAR. Kidding. 'The cow jumped over the moon.'

MARIA. 'The little dog laughed to see such sport.'

ALL. 'And the dish ran away with the spoon!'

MARIA. Is Your Mama a Llama?

STEF. Are You My Mother?

MARIA. Brown Bear, Brown Bear, What do you see?

STEF. Why so many questions, anyway? Oy!

CHAR. There's always The Big Red Barn

MARIA. Chicka Chicka ABC

CHAR. Go Dog Go

MARIA. Pat the Bunny

CHAR. Pat the Cat

STEF. Pat the Puppy

MARIA. The Little Engine That Could

CHAR. Freight Train

STEF. Jamberry

MARIA. Goodnight Gorilla

CHAR. If You Give a Mouse a Cookie

STEF. If You Give a Pig a Pancake

MARIA. If You Give a Moose a Muffin

ALL. AAAAARRRGGGHHHH!!!

CHAR. Stop the madness .... !

MARIA. If I read The Cat in the Hat one more time ...

STEF. You know, reading books for a jillion times is bad enough, but what about the songs???

CHAR. Ohmygawd. To think I used to sing Sondheim, Gershwin, Cole Porter and now I sing...

MARIA. *(singing)* Twinkle Twinkle Little Star

CHAR. *(singing as a round)* Baa Baa Black Sheep Have You Any Wool

STEF. *(joining in the round)* A B C D E F G

ALL. Same tune!!

MARIA. There are really only two melodies for all the children's music in the world you know.

CHAR. Right - **(SINGING AGAIN)** ... This old man, he played one, he played knick knack on his thumb ...

STEF. *(singing)* I love you, you love me, we're a happy family ...

MARIA. This is beyond pathetic – what have we come to? *(singing as she walks off)* The itsy bitsy spider went up the water spout ...

CHAR & STEF. *(singing also – same tune!)* Little Bunny Foo Foo, hopping through the forest...

(They exit. Back to **ELLEN**.*)*

ELLEN. I have always been a kind of over-the-top, wear-my-heart-on-my sleeve person. And I've always been hypersensitive about certain things. But nothing in my life prepared me for the emotional juggernaut that would be my brain after I had my first baby. I mean everything associated with him took on this hyper-resonance and deeper meaning. Things which I had no business thinking about suddenly became fodder for analysis worthy of Jung or Freud. And it was not necessarily about life's big issues. It was about the words to lullabies, for instance. I started to sing my new baby that old standby – Rockabye Baby. *(sings a little)* "Rockabye baby, on the treetop…" and I'm thinking to myself, as I hold my son, VERY late one long night… "As the bough breaks, the cradle will FALL? AND DOWN WILL COME BABY, CRADLE AND ALL???" This is not a good song for a paranoid new mother to be crooning to her vulnerable little infant. So, I changed the lyrics! Swear to gawd. It became "As the bough breaks/ the cradle will, *stay*, and there will lie baby/ *sleeping away…*" Even wrote them in over the old lyrics in a song book. I mean, if this kind of behavior doesn't make me eligible for a lifetime supply of Valium, I don't know what would. But it didn't stop there. I started reading fairy tale books to my son and I'm wondering about the three little pigs, who are pretty vicious when they fry the big bad wolf in a pot of water at the end. And what about that giant that eats little children? Is this good bedtime reading? I THINK NOT! And what's up with the other nursery rhymes? *(singing brutally)* "They all ran after the farmer's wife who cut off their tails with a butcher's knife…" Except somehow I didn't remember the part about the butcher's knife from my childhood. All I remembered was *(singing again sweetly)* "They all ran after the farmer's wife, you've never seen such a sight in your life…" Now-why-is-that? And then it hits me – OHMYGAWD.

My mother was insane too and she changed the lyrics for me... (**ELLEN** *exits.*)

(**STEF** *enters.*)

STEF. Mom? It's me...Everyone's great...Really...Sounds corny, but she is so incredibly beautiful, I love her so much...just the shape of her head, the way she sleeps with her fists all tight, the sound of her low little voice...Makes catching vomit in my hand a not-big deal...I love you Mom, thanks for listening... (**STEF** *sits on the bench.*)

(**CHARLOTTE** *enters.*)

CHAR. The whole thing is beyond words – beyond expectation...Being a mom is a daily dose of...well, the agony and the ecstasy. It's a perfect job for a manic depressive...your moods swing from the highest of euphoria one minute to the depths of despair in the next... One thing I finally learned was not to be too cocky or too insecure as a parent no matter what is going on... Whether it's great or horrible, it won't last... Your baby sleeps through the night at two weeks? Just wait till she gets to the terrible two's... Late talker? Early walker... Knows his A-B-C's at a year and a half? Won't tie his shoes until he's seven... You just have to ride a lot of it out – the good, the bad and the ugly. But you know what – it is quite simply, the best thing I have ever done.... (**CHARLOTTE** *sits down right* – **ELLEN** *enters.*)

ELLEN. Having children is 80% frustration and 20% joy, and even though mathematically, and logically, it makes no sense, somehow the 20% completely makes up for the 80%.

(**ELLEN** *sits up left* – **MARIA** *enters.*)

MARIA. For some reason, being a mother reminds me of a *Gilligan's Island* rerun...It's the one where the radioactive fruits and vegetables wash up on the beach, and the characters who eat them show hugely exaggerated effects....Mary Ann eats carrots, and she spots a yacht a billion miles offshore, Lovey eats the sugar beets and buzzes around like she's on amphetamines, and someone else eats spinach and rips out a tree or something...Anyway this episode made me think about being a mother. Because when it comes to my child, all of my emotions are hugely exaggerated. As if I before I had I child, I was walking around only half understanding emotions, since they affected me alone. And then I ate up all the radioactive fruits and now suffer and enjoy the full range of those emotions...love, joy, pain, pride and terror... I thought I knew all about love, and then I had my little boy and it was just like when the Grinch hears the Whos down in Whoville singing and his heart grows so big it busts out of that little frame. And I thought I knew fear before, until I watched my nine week old having a spinal tap, so dehydrated that his lips were cracked and no tears came with the screams. And joy, until I first held my newborn baby... It is, by miles and miles, the most important thing I've done. The most wonderful, awful, scary, overwhelming, fulfilling, depleting and enriching thing I've done...

CHAR. *(pulling out a pregnancy test stick and checking her watch:)* Oh my gawd, it's blue again!

(blackout)

(Pre-show music comes up for intermission.)

ACT II

(Three of the moms walk onstage:)

MARIA. So, we had made it through the first year as new parents... We'd all survived, more or less. And we realized it was time to start "trying" again. Except this time it didn't happen just like that... We were just so tired from working and doing and the exhaustion of first time parenting... My husband and I would look at each other and grumble, "Time to make the Baby" like the Dunkin Donuts commercial. We'd do it. Trying hard to relax, but anxious to get it done and move on. Throw my legs in the air – because someone said that's what you should do and pray to regain my dignity once this is all over...

STEF. Who knew I'd never again go to the bathroom by myself? Eat an entire piece of ANYTHING without having to give SOMEONE a bite? Get yanked about by the arm by my toddler who knows just what she wants but can't reach it? I began to really miss work, where I could get to the end of the day feeling like I'd accomplished something, even if it was just getting a memo out, or could actually eat lunch when I was hungry. With my newborn, just making it to the end of the day alive was an accomplishment, and it was a banner day if I got dressed, too. Then having TWO little kids took over my life, my house, in ways I never imagined... I remember a friend once telling me about stopping back at her house to change her clothes after dropping her kids off at daycare, and bursting into tears because she was so happy to be ALONE in her bedroom, without someone pulling at her, crying, grabbing her things. And just how pathetic that was... I had no idea what she meant at the time... But I do now.

CHAR. I don't think my first child heard me raise my voice for her first year and a half of life... Until my second child was born...I mean that first year or so as a mom was really magic. Sure I was scared and nervous for a lot of it, and the sleep deprivation was no fun, to say nothing of "tough love weekend..." You know, when you let your baby cry it out so that she'll sleep through the night... But I had so much patience and time just for her. I was able to do it all right, more or less, and the overwhelming sense of love for her just amazed me. Everyone was always saying what a good mother I was, and how patient I was, and I felt good about it. I have to admit, painful thought that it is, I spent some time congratulating myself on doing it right. I mean, I did and I guess I still do, but believe me, I'm not nearly as smug as I was as a parent of one lovable baby. When I got pregnant with our second child, I wondered how I could possibly love another child as much as my first. And how hard it would be for my first kid to adjust... And, my second child was born, and I fell in love with her instantly, and immediately started to lose my patience with the first little princess... But it's all worked out somehow. Although I sometimes miss the magic moments of being mommy to just one child.

(**STEF, MARIA** and **CHARLOTTE** *exit.* **ELLEN** *walks on.*)

ELLEN. So, here I am, this mother of two toddlers, pregnant with the third, house in the suburbs, minivan on order, and just a hair's breadth away from losing my mind. Now on the one hand, the kids keep me busy and running all day, never a minute to myself. On the other hand, when my universe has been tightened to focus on two little kids and all their needs and wants... Well, I get lonely... I want companionship... Someone to talk to with whom I have a lot in common. Someone to share good times and bad.... So what do I do? Start picking up strange women on the playground...I mean, really, any suburban playground is just a singles bar with different characters...

We're all there – checking each other out, deciding who looks like a potential candidate and who doesn't, whether their kids would be a good match with yours. And then I make my move. I have, of course, my standard opening lines: "Are you using this swing?", "How old is your son?", "Do you come here often?" I feel my way through the conversation and the whole time I'm thinking, "Should I ask for her phone number? Set-up a playdate? Am I her type?" I get the nerve up and exchange numbers, and just pray that there'll be some sort of compatibility among moms and kids for the first "date." I wait a few days, so I don't seem too anxious and make the call. I leave a message and wait for the call back. She calls! I set it up for a week from now and make it casual and fun. Then she arrives with her kids, and we spend the whole time talking in broken sentences and bitching about motherhood. But that's a whole different story...

(**ELLEN** *walks into the next scene to join* **CHARLOTTE, MARIA** *and* **STEFANIE** *on chairs.*)

CHAR. Come on in – we're just getting settled...

M&S. Hey...hi...etc.

STEF. We were just being catty about other mothers who drive us crazy at the playground. It's awful but you have to vent sometimes, right?

CHAR. Like the one that drives me crazy is the "show-off Mom." You know, the one who is talking in just enough of a loud voice so we can all hear what a great mom she is and how wonderful her child is..."Ooohh, honey, what a goood job you are doing, what a good, good boy, Mommy just loves you so, so much......

MARIA. I know! And the one that gets me is the "nurturing Mom" who has the patience of Job, and makes you feel this big for screaming at your child ever. You know, kind've crunchy granola, sweet, tolerant voice, always patient – you just want to slap her silly.

CHAR. Or the saccharin sweet mother I see at Dunkin' Donuts. Like something out of a fucking Talbot's catalogue, all matchy-matchy with the kids...So then the little boy in a Ralph Lauren suspender outfit starts up on the sister. And I hear the mother, just a little too loud as usual,

STEF. ...as if the world will benefit from listening to her...

CHAR. "Now Tyler, we don't hurt one another in our family, do we? How do you think Courtney feels when you smack her head?"

STEF. "I think you're angry little love-bug."

ELLEN. "Why don't you try to use your words honey?"

STEF. "It makes mommy sad inside to see you hurt your sister."

CHAR. EXACTLY! And all I want her to do is to grab the little shit, skip the sprinkly donut, go back to fairyland or wherever the hell they live...

ELLEN. Maybe even yell at him...

STEF. What about the "absentee mom?" When her little monster is hogging the swings and verbally abusing your child she's off sitting on the bench...

MARIA. ...reading People or filing her nails...

STEF. It's like, "Listen kid, where's your mother?"

CHAR. How about the moms with their first child, around ten months, hair in a little ribbon...

STEF. ...clean cutesy outfit...

CHAR. ...and they still think...

MARIA. ...the whole world is in love with their child...

STEF. Remember having one child?

ELLEN. Kind of... I think it is true about two kids being three times as hard as one...

MARIA. Try having three kids in four years...

ELLEN. Yikes...

CHAR. Or having twins as your second child...

MARIA. Two boys is four times more work than two girls...

STEF. I think boys are easier than girls ..

CHAR. No way – girls are much easier….

MARIA. C'mon – it's the oldest that's the easiest – whether it's a boy or girl…

STEF. No, no, the second is a piece of cake because you are so much more relaxed…

MARIA. HA – my second has been the high maintenance child since birth…

ELLEN. I didn't mean to start something…

CHAR. OK girls, we've done it again "the Mommy Olympics" – who has it the worst…

STEF. No, I shouldn't complain. My kids are really great.

MARIA. Mine too – I'm so lucky. We all are…you have the moments where you can step back away from it all and count your blessings but there's a lot more moments when you are pulling your hair out.

STEF. Yeah, it's peck, peck peck all day. Like chickens working their way across the barnyard….

CHAR. …like Tippi Hedren in *The Birds*…

MARIA. Oh please, I'm Charlie Brown and my kids are Lucy, pulling the football out from underneath me…

ELLEN. Yeah, but there are those good moments, too…

CHAR. No, you're right. Like those great moments, when you finally stop whatever nonsense you are doing and sit on the floor with them, and just play and laugh and think – oh my god, they are so beautiful and you think, this is it, this makes it all okay….

ELLEN. Or when you can all snuggle together for a few minutes, and read a book that everyone likes, and everyone can listen to, without fighting about it…

MARIA. I love when I can just sit in a rocking chair and hold my youngest, and look at him and marvel at him and remember how awesome it felt to hold him as a baby. Although there's a part of me that wouldn't go back to the newborn thing if you paid me…

STEF. Not me, I love little babies, that's my favorite part, when they are so dependent and cuddly and can't talk back – or spit at you…

CHAR. Spitting…? Pinching – whining – crying… taking – taking – taking… aaaaggghghghgh!

MARIA. *(to* **STEF.** *about* **CHARLOTTE***)* Have we lost her do you think?

STEF. No, I think she's still with us, but she's hanging by a thread…

CHAR. Nothing that a little Zoloft couldn't cure…

STEF. Lifetime supply of Valium is what I say…

MARIA. No, a little Morphine drip in the kitchen, right next to the coffeemaker, that you can go to whenever you need it. Beep, beep…

ELLEN. Oh yeah. Just trying to keep it together. The thing I don't get is how do you do it all? I mean there's just so much to do…

CHAR. You lower your standards.

STEF. Absolutely. I remember when I had my first baby I was feeling swallowed up. And then I surrendered. To a house not so clean…

CHAR. …to a pile of unread Newsweek magazines…

MARIA. …to legs in need of a shave…

CHAR. To making dinner that's not really "dinner"….

MARIA. But is microwave mac and cheese…

ELLEN. Frozen waffles…

CHAR. …cheese balls and juice boxes…

MARIA. And in general, a relaxation of rules. With our first child, my husband and I were over the edge with paranoia. I stuck the baby monitor right next to his face and one night he gets the hiccups – oh no! So my husband and I get up at three a.m., and each grabbed baby books for advice on the hiccups. Two masters' degrees between us, so we figure the answer MUST be in a book, right? But of course there is no answer. They were the HICCUPS! And after about 10 more of these incidents, I had to let go... After my third child, the baby monitor was stuffed in a drawer...

ELLEN. Yeah, with my first, a temperature of ninety-nine would send me rushing to the phone to call the doctor... Now it's like – have some Tylenol, you'll be fine...

STEF. I knew I had arrived as a mother when I could deal simultaneously with vomit and diarrhea and not freak out...

(Everyone gets up to leave – ad lib off as chairs go back in place.)

*(**MOMS** exit except **CHARLOTTE**.)*

CHAR. When my daughter was ten months old, she got some horrific stomach virus... This was the big leagues... fifteen diapers a day, rash on her butt as red as hot-house tomatoes, Pedialyte by the gallon and it went on and on and on... Of course, she gets dehydrated and is admitted to Children's Hospital. It took three long days and nights to figure out she was really fine after all. But not before I went through all my clean clothes, underwear included, my fake nails snapped off, my hair was up in a ponytail and my eyes look like fucking dime-slots... So I'm wearing hospital scrubs and trying to keep it together.... I called home to check in with my husband and my other two kids, and put on my best Florence Henderson Wessonality voice. It sounded too high and cheerful even to me, but I couldn't seem to rein it in... I promised, "We're fine and I'll bring the world's yummiest lollipops home soon." Like lollipops will make all the fucking difference... So, we finally get to go home... My husband and other children come to get us and we're driving home – and my oldest gets carsick. All over the back of the van... I empty out the bucket 'o pretzels, scrambling like a football running back through the van. On the way, I catch a look at my still sick baby. I vaguely register hearing a Mom? Mom? Mom? Mom.. from the third child, the only healthy one…. until she gets louder, insistent over the cries of the vomiting sister and the sick baby – MOM! MOM! MOOOOOOOMMM… What?…I finally scream at her WHAT DO YOU WANT???? To which my sweet little girl says, "I just want my fucking lollipop!"…Where the fuck did she get that?

(CHARLOTTE exits. ELLEN enters downstage of table.)

ELLEN. There really should be a twelve-step program for mothers. You know, in the list of compulsions – drinking, gambling, shopping – you would just have to add motherhood. You talk about needing recovery! Your playgroup could form an intervention to get you in. Or, even better, the hospital could put discreet information in the diaper bag on the way home with your local chapter listed. A New Way of Life. The Fellowship of Group Meetings. There is no group on earth that needs that kind of support more than mothers. Think about it, Mothers Anonymous – or "MA." Hello, my name is – uh, Trixie, and I am a mother. Easy Does It. One Day at a Time. The Serenity Prayer. I could have a sponsor, someone to call when I hit bottom and am about to inflict semi-permanent psychic damage on my young children. I could learn about co-dependency and enabling. If I go on a binge of awful parenting, I quickly hit a meeting, secure in my anonymity. And okay, maybe there's not twelve-steps – who has the time? Maybe just three-steps for moms. And on-site babysitting. And you would have to SERVE WINE and crudité instead of coffee and snacks. As soon as my kids are in school, I'm forming the first chapter.

(ELLEN exits, STEFANIE enters down left.)

STEF. So during one very long week of motherhood I had to go to Wal-Mart with my son and youngest daughter to load up on various things, including presents for my son's birthday. So, at the entrance to Wal-Mart I stop to ask for their cooperation and help getting through the store. *This is to a three year old and a four year old…*

Piece of cake, right?…The cart is too small for them to ride in so we are making our way through the aisles and I'm frantically throwing supplies in, hoping to get everything I need before a major melt down. My daughter is so not cooperating… By aisle three, the cart was full and I had already exhausted the *full range of behavior modification techniques.* I had tried positive reinforcement, negative reinforcement, the carrot, the stick, pleading, yelling, begging, whispering, kind words, angry words and various threats. In aisle four, I give up and kneel down to have the big talk with the little…. My son, in the meantime, is fiddling around with the shelves behind me and says in a calm voice "Mommy, my thumb is stuck." Without taking my eyes off the offending child, I say, "So pull your thumb out." "Mommy, I can't." I whip around and sort of semi-yank his thumb out of the tiny metal hole he has stuck it in and oops – blood….Gushing blood… Not so bad as to alert Wal-Mart personnel but not so great looking either. I frantically start digging through the cart looking for the wipes from aisle two while trying to shield my son's vision from the birthday gift I had surreptitiously slipped into the cart. I find the wipes, rip open the package, apply pressure and pick up my son. Holding him in one arm, barking orders to my daughter and pushing the overflowing cart with my elbow, I make my way through the aisles, trying to find the Band-Aids and Neosporin. I find I can't stop myself from continuing to throw stuff into the cart – oh look – a great deal on tissues – that's the carpet cleaner I've been looking for. This is insanity… I am insane… Something… Find the Band-Aids and Neosporin, apply copious amounts of both to the bleeding appendage, drag both kids to the checkout counter and then to the car, yelling instructions and threats the whole way, load everyone in, start the car and burst into tears. Just another glamorous, fulfilling hour of motherhood.

(STEF. *exits.* **CHARLOTTE** *and* **ELLEN** *at Starbucks again.*)

CHAR. Ok, I've got my non-fat venti mocha Frappucino, I'm good.

ELLEN. Yeah, I'm skipping the cream cheese brownie these days. Trying to lose that "baby fat" – the fat caused by HAVING a baby!

CHAR. Hey you know, nine months on, nine months off.

ELLEN. Yeah, I had decided to give myself a year, till his first birthday.

CHAR. And how's it going?

ELLEN. He just turned two.

CHAR. I kept getting down to within ten pounds and then I'd get pregnant again. So each time, I've added 10 more pounds to the overall net weight gain... Do the math...

ELLEN. I've been on a diet, since, well, puberty. I'm trying to help my kids avoid all my food baggage. You know the stress eating, the guilt eating...

CHAR. Yeah, I hear you. I don't know a single woman who doesn't have "food issues," something I SWORE I would never pass on to my daughters. And yet my kids are like poster children for the phrase "picky eater." One only eats bread products and they live on mac and cheese.

ELLEN. Oh, if I make the "cheesiest" one more time, the Kraft people are going to give me a reward...

CHAR. ...The bar is pretty damn low when you are counting corn muffins and banana bread in the five servings a day group.

ELLEN. My three year-old doesn't eat fruit, doesn't eat vegetables and won't eat any meat. No fish sticks, no chicken nuggets, nothing...

CHAR. So what does he eat for dinner?

ELLEN. A Sesame Street vitamin and some Cheerios.

CHAR. That's all you give him?

ELLEN. No, that's all he'll eat, no matter what I put in front
of him. I have grated carrots into meatloaf and made
happy faces out of broccoli and tomatoes. Like that
works... I have even caught myself using those hokey
phrases my mother used on me: "Eat your crusts,
they'll make your hair curly," and "You know, there
are children starving in Botswana"... Nothing works,
never does.

CHAR. Yeah, it's a daily exercise in futility – the only exercise I get actually...

ELLEN. When I really want my kids to eat we do breakfast
for dinner...pancakes, waffles, whatever...

CHAR. I've totally given up as the food Nazi. Now that I've
waved the white flag on food, my next challenge is getting some romance back in my life with my husband...

ELLEN. Oh right, romance. I think that went out with the
placenta. After three children, my body has never been
the same again. Stretch marks everywhere, droopy
boobs – I don't want to see my ugly-ass self naked,
much less share how I look with my husband.

CHAR. Ain't it the truth? It's so hard to feel sexy when
my breasts and ass have been stretched beyond their
limits... Not that there's actually TIME for sex, mind
you...

ELLEN. Yeah, after spending all day being grabbed at by
little sticky hands, I can't even think of letting one
more human being touch me.

CHAR. Oh, I totally relate. But I have a friend who's been
married twice, and she tells me that after having her
second child, she's having the best sex of her life. I
go, honey, that's about having *a second husband*, not a
second child....

ELLEN. Maybe I should get one of those...

CHAR. Then he'd have to see your ass...

(CHAR *and* ELLEN *exit.* MARIA *walks on, at bench area.*)

MARIA. With girls, you worry about confidence issues, eating disorders, catty friends, all that stuff. I was a girl once so I knew. But when I had two boys, I realized it was going to be a whole new world for me. Anyone with both boys and girls will tell you they are wired differently. The testosterone thing just happens. For instance, the peeing thing… This is not something that I knew about myself as a young child because I didn't pee from a… Part of our success in toilet training my youngest son was to let him go outside. He really liked it… Boys…well… Of course, his pre-school had to call me about him peeing in the playground at recess… So, my mother's group decides to have the kids meet after school for lunch and play at a local playground. Everything was going great. I was enjoying lunch with the other moms, the kids were playing nicely when I look over and my son is peeing, in a large arc, over the seesaw and hitting a tree. On my way over to stop him, another boy in the class drops drawer and pees the same way, trying to arc higher. All the other kids, especially the girls, are staring. The proverbial pissing contest…At age three.

(MARIA *exits.* STEF. *walks on, sits on the chair backwards, down center.*)

STEF. So how do you think the Tooth Fairy writes? I'm guessing little circles to dot her I's. And a lotta swirly letters. So here I go perpetuating a big lie. The Tooth Fairy. The Easter Bunny. Santa Claus. You know. My daughter lost a tooth. She's five years old, so I'm excited because this is a milestone, she's growing up, getting big girl teeth, all of that. But she jumps on the Tooth Fairy thing right away…getting psyched about the money. Five bucks for the first tooth in our house… Only the first one. But after she's psyched about the Tooth Fairy, she starts asking questions. Like when does she come. How does she get in the house. How come the kids don't wake up when she takes the tooth from under the pillow. What does she do with all those teeth. And then she starts to freak out. I can see her face change.

A fairy? Coming in my HOUSE? Reaching under my PILLOW? What the hell kind of deal is this? And then she starts to cry, so I concoct this plot where we stick her tooth outside in the mailbox, and then the Tooth Fairy would leave the money out there, with a note of course. But then I realized I didn't have any cash. I was going to use a mall gift certificate, until a neighbor coughed up some money. Jesus. So why didn't I just tell her there's no such thing? I really wanted to. But it's bigger than me, you know? She's only five, so if I tell her, she'll tell the kids on the bus. The kids in the neighborhood. And then I've got an angry mob of parents who actually LIKE this stuff mad at me for blowing their cover. Sounds like a conspiracy. Which it IS! Busy elves, bunnies hopping down the street. A big fat guy getting down the chimney? And all of the pretend magic, which goes bust the minute you tell them. I remember finding out there was no Santa, and then, like dream dominoes, down falls the bunny, the fairy, all of them. And up comes the realization that you've been lied to. By your parents, and teachers and everyone. And for what? Isn't there enough real stuff for her to go through, without this made up nonsense? I mean she's going to be excluded by a group of girls someday. And dumped by a guy. And have the agony of childbirth. And lose a good, true friend. And fail herself. And stand at the wake of her father and me...So that's why I don't feel like lying about the Tooth Fairy. It won't make the real pain better, but she won't have suffered stupidly, on things I could have spared her. I guess that's it, really....

(STEF. walks into next scene with her chair, joins ELLEN, CHARLOTTE and MARIA who have pulled chairs down center.)

MARIA. You know, I love books and I love reading and obviously this is something I wanted to pass on to my children. So, when my son was born, I dutifully started the nighttime ritual – even though he was about two months old and couldn't have cared less.

ELLEN. Didn't you feel a little ridiculous sitting there and reading *Goodnight Moon* to a six week-old baby?

CHAR. Yeah – gotta get the reading part of the brain working – the things I read to my daughter…

STEF. Between three children over the past six years I've now read like 9,260 children's books.

CHAR. And aren't some so awful that you can barely stand to read them?

ELLEN. Or how about when you're tired and you secretly skip over words or pages to get to the end quicker…

STEF. How about when they catch you doing that?

MARIA. How about getting jealous of the characters you are reading about? You see a character sitting on the beach reading – and you think – I'd love to do that for just one day. Except the really pathetic part is…

CHAR. …that the character is an orange dinosaur.

MARIA. …So you're jealous of an orange dinosaur in a book with three sappy words on each page. It doesn't get much lower than that…

ELLEN. I just hate when it's been a long day, and they pick out the two books you hate the most and they are reaaaallly loooong ones….

STEF. Oh, you let them pick out their own books?

MARIA. *(sarcastically)* Uh, yeah! Why, what do you do?

STEF. OK, I know I'm the biggest nerd, but I always go upstairs sometime before dinner, and pick out three books for each kid…

CHAR. …Cut it out

STEF. …And leave them out for bedtime. I just can't fight another battle with them at that point, and I guess I just want to read them what I want to read them…

CHAR. OK, Miss Scary Anal Person…

ELLEN. Hey, actually that's not bad, I might try that…

STEF. I've just gotten so I know I can't control a lot, but what I can control I need to… I just really miss, really long for those things that are gone forever, or at least it feels like forever.

ELLEN. Like going shopping by yourself...

MARIA. ...or going out at night without being in a panic about the new babysitter, and what it costs, and how your kids will act for the babysitter...

STEF. ...and I better be home by a certain time because she's only thirteen and she has school tomorrow...

ELLEN. And yet, we're supposed to "cherish this time with our children"...

CHAR. Yeah, I cherish them, I cherish them when they are ASLEEP – IN THEIR BEDS – AT NIGHT, looking like little angels, instead of...

STEF. ...during the day, when you know this is everything you ever wanted, and you should be counting all your blessings, but instead you just want to go...

ELLEN. ...quietly, permanently insane...

MARIA. I can't believe what I hear myself saying, sometimes over and over again...

CHAR. You mean please may I have some more?

MARIA. Don't talk with your mouth full.

STEF. *(walks downstage, playing out)* I'll be there IN A MINUTE.

ELLEN. *(walks downstage, playing out)* Not right now...

CHAR. *(walks downstage, playing out)* What do you mean you burped in your underwear?

MARIA. *(walks downstage, next to **CHARLOTTE**, plays out)* Don't touch yourself down there; you'll get an infection.

CHAR. *(to **MARIA**)* You didn't say that!

MARIA. *(to **CHARLOTTE**)* Okay, only once, and I regretted it.

STEF. Let's play a game! Let's see who can be quiet the longest!

ELLEN. Face over the plate, chew with your mouth closed.

CHAR. *(back to playing out)* It is not okay to hit your brother.

MARIA. *(back to playing out)* Use words please.

STEF. We'll see...

MARIA. I need you to listen.

CHAR. Daddy doesn't have a tail, honey – it's a penis and all boys have them.

ELLEN. No honey, it's Corn Pops, not Porn Cops.

STEF. Put the tissue over your nose before you blow.

MARIA. Food is for eating, not for playing.

CHAR. You mean "please."

ELLEN. I didn't hear "please."

STEF. Why is it that you ask them to say please every single day and they never remember, and yet, if you say "shit" ONE TIME, they can't stop saying it to you?

CHAR. If I say "you'll have to wait a minute" one more time…

STEF. IN A MINUTE.

MARIA. NOT RIGHT NOW.

CHAR. Keep your hands where they are supposed to be.

STEF. I'm only one person.

ELLEN. Because sleeping in the same bed helps Mommy & Daddy keep warm.

STEF. I'm so proud of you – You DID it!!!

CHAR. So tell me again? When you grow up there are no motorcycles, no cigarettes, no body piercing, no far away colleges. Very Good.

STEF. I'll always love you.

ELLEN. No matter what.

CHAR. Even when you're naughty.

MARIA. Even when you're not being nice

STEF. I'm going to count to three….

MARIA. Wipe front first, then back.

STEF. One…

ELLEN. Wipe until you don't see anything, okay?

STEF. Two:

CHAR. I'll give you two choices…

STEF. Two and a half…

MARIA. For me? I love your drawing!

CHAR. You are so smart!

STEF. Two and three quarters…

ELLEN. That's great honey!

MARIA. Because!

CHAR. The kitchen's closed.

STEF. TEETH HAIR BEDS BACKPACKS… Let's go people!

ELLEN. When you are grown-up you can do it your way.

STEF. Don't make me come up there…

CHAR. How many times do I have to tell you?

MARIA. Can you all just stop fighting for a few minutes!

ELLEN. I REALLY MEAN IT!

CHAR. When you're a mom, you can do it your way.

ELLEN. Someday you'll understand…

MARIA. This hurts me more than it hurts you…

STEF. Because you just have to…

CHAR. Because I said so…

MARIA. Because I'm the mom!

(**ELLEN, CHARLOTTE** and **STEFANIE** walk off, leaving **MARIA** down right.

There are times in your life when everything is going along smoothly and more or less happily, and you're in a good rhythm, and suddenly the earth tilts, and the world as you know it just disappears. And so it happens the day you walk into a department store and lose your child… From the moment they begin to move, your children take your constant attention and focus. It's as if you develop a third eye, this heightened sense of where your children are and what danger they're about to get into. So I was not afraid of walking into the crowded store just before lunchtime, with my two year-old. I knew he liked to look at the colors and touch the clothes, but he usually stayed right with me, and I'm a good mom, I would keep a close eye on him. And then my attention wandered for maybe a millisecond, and when I turned around, he was gone.

I mean, absolutely nowhere in sight. I did a quick sweep with my eyes before the bottom dropped out of my stomach, and my heart lurched violently. A dozen nasty scenarios flashed through my brain: the child-less woman who always wanted a little boy, the predator hanging around kids' stores just waiting for an unat-tended child to wander... I called his name, fear in my voice; no answer. Frantically, I began searching up and down aisles, looking at other moms as I tore through the racks, calling his name louder and louder, sure he would appear at any moment, and just as sure that he was gone... I started to cry as I called again and again, and just as I thought my heart would burst, there he was, humming happily under a round rack of clothes, totally oblivious to my terrifying search. Relief flooded my body, my legs went like jelly. The whole episode had lasted about a minute and a half, but it felt like a lifetime, and I know I aged ten years.

(**MARIA** *crosses to the bench,* **ELLEN** *enters.*)

ELLEN. From the moment my first child was born, all my lifelong tendencies toward neurotic, worst-case scenar-ios became exacerbated – to an excruciating point. I mean the emotion and love I felt for this little girl, and the protective maternal instinct, just served to make my fear of "when bad things happen to good people" bubble over and come this close to exploding... But I tried to maintain a grip, and after the first year and the first child it got a little easier... And after success-fully bringing my kids through the gamut of baby and toddler illnesses and accidents, I began to let go a little and convince myself that it was all going to be OK... But chronic habitual paranoia doesn't die easily... So, one day I am putting sunscreen on my kids and I notice a raised dark red bruise on the back of my daughter's thigh. Got to be some sort of horrible disease causing it, right? It wasn't a regular bruise, and it was isolated and not in any place that she could've bumped or hit. My mind leaped through all the various scenarios – my husband and me pacing the halls at Children's Hospital, family members arriving to take care of my other kids, concerned medical staff, bike rides organized as fund-raisers, e-mails sent to caring friends, the whole nine yards – I've got it all played out. Then we go outside and my husband joins us and I ask him to take a look at it in the sun. And he does, and all of a sudden I hear my daughter say, "Stop Daddy, that hurts" and I look over and my husband says to me: cherry bubblegum. CHERRY BUBBLEGUM. And it's gone, and obviously, so is my mind...

*(**ELLEN** crosses to table up left, **CHARLOTTE** enters.)*

CHAR. Tubal ligation. Sounds more like a ride at Water Country than a surgical procedure. Come on down to Water Country and ride our newest thrill sensation... the Tubal Ligation! And be ready for FUN! Not. I had it done a month after giving birth. And most of me is relieved. Phew! Three healthy children, no more pregnancies, no more birth control, all set. Onto the next chapter. I'm 43, I mean really! So this is our house, this is it. These are the three people I will know to my core. No others. No more seeing a face for the first time. No more feeling life inside me. No more telling people you love that a new baby is on the way. No more letting someone feel the baby kick. No more smelling the baby's head, no more tiny toes to kiss, no more of any of it. So I know it was right, and I know I am blessed, but I can't help but wonder who else might have joined us if I skipped my ride on the Tubal Ligation. Who else I could have loved so truly.

*(**CHARLOTTE** moves stage right – **STEFANIE** enters to center stage.)*

STEF. In one way, I was so excited to see the end of the summer, that I was sending my oldest daughter to school – real school – finally. I could face a day without the silent inventory of what's up my sleeve if she and my other kids got whiny or bored...are they reading enough, playing with each other, what about sunscreen and manners and learning and fun, dammit, we've got to have fun... So the day comes for my oldest daughter to go on the bus to all day first grade. I stood at the bus stop with the fresh-faced neighbor kids with their new shoes, and the parents, all of us with cameras – and the rush of the new year in the air... I saw my daughter's back go up the steps onto the bus, her eyes casting just a brief glance my way as she happily took her seat. And I felt the rush of panic seize me... what if she's not ready? What if she's too shy? What if the girls are mean? Girls can be so mean...what if the bus crashes on the way? Why aren't there seat belts on the bus? The white hot thoughts whiz through my mind without prompting like some sick newsreel, and all the while this frozen smile is pasted on my face so she doesn't see that I'm scared. Terrified, really. Because she's leaving me a little today. And there's a whole part of her that's not mine to know; the little girl that's on the bus, and at school, and at lunch and on the playground. Her own self, hardly molded, not yet set. I need more time. I'm sure I didn't do it right. She isn't ready yet... And then, with the psycho cheer pasted on my face, and the hand at the end of my arm waving, I throw up into my mouth and go home and cry hard for a long time.

*(Fade to black as something like Natalie Cole's "This Will Be (An Everlasting Love)" comes up for the curtain call.)**

(**Note:** *In the original production at the ICA Boston in 2002, for the closing performance, we put together a Power Point of photos of all of our kids, starting with an ultrasound and leading up through the age where they go to kindergarten, with a music underscore. We only did this once, because the moms who watch this show feel as though we are talking about their lives, and their kids and we didn't want to be specific about our kids, except for that one time. After all, it's because of our kids that we wrote the show.)*

** Please see Music Use Note on Page 3.

SET PIECES

Act 1: Four chairs, two small tables, one round table, one park bench, two quilt wall hangings

Act II: Four chairs, one round table, one park bench, two quilt wall hangings

Costume note: the characters evolve from business/professional/fashionable clothes at the top of the show to maternity clothes to mom clothes, except for Maria who goes back to business clothes once she 'goes back to work'(vibrator monologue). This can be accomplished in whatever simple or more complex way the director chooses. Generally speaking, the less costume changes the better because of the flow of the show. Obviously a lot can be done with accessories – or lack thereof as the case may be.

ACT I

Costume pieces:	Props:
Stefanie	
Dark blue pants	Briefcase
Rose button down shirt	Cell phone
Dark blue jacket	Hospital phone
Pregnancy pillow	Ice pack
Pink maternity shirt	
Bathrobe, slippers	
T-shirt	
Charlotte	
Black pants	Briefcase
Rust top	Digital thermometer
Black jacket	Starbucks coffee cup
Pregnancy pillow	"What to Expect" book
Maternity top	
Black and gold striped top	
Maria	
Black pants	Briefcase
Light blue sweater set	Day planner
Pregnancy pillow	
Blue maternity top	
Blue button front shirt	
T-shirt, zip front sweat shirt	
Ellen	
Black pants	Large handbag
Blue top	Starbucks coffee cup
Pregnancy pillow	Photo album and photos
Green maternity shirt	
Blue button down shirt	

ACT II

Costume pieces:	Props:

Stefanie
Black pants — Wine glass
Peach sweater

Charlotte
Grey pants — Wine glass
Tan sweater — Starbucks coffee cup

Maria
Black pants — Wine glass
Blue sweater

Ellen
Maternity jeans
Navy maternity top
Brown pants — Wine glass
Dark brown sweater — Starbucks coffee cup

OTHER TITLES AVAILABLE FROM SAMUEL FRENCH

HATS! THE MUSICAL

Book by Marcia Milgrom Dodge & Anthony Dodge.
Additional Material by Rob Bartlett, Lynne Taylor-Corbett &
Sharon Vaughn. Songs by Doug Besterman, Susan Birkenhead,
Michele Brourman, Pat Bunch, Gretchen Cryer, Anthony Dodge,
Marcia Milgrom Dodge, Beth Falcone, David Friedman, Kathie
Lee Gifford, David Goldsmith, Carol Hall, Henry Krieger, Stephen
Lawrence, Melissa Manchester, Amanda McBroom, Pam Tillis &
Sharon Vaughn.

Musical Comedy / 7f

Exploding with fun, *Hats!* is a new musical about a 49.999 year-old
woman who reluctantly faces the inevitable BIG 5-0…until she meets
several remarkable women who show her about fun, friendship and
forgetting about things that simply don't matter anymore.

Hats! features original music by a team of Grammy®, Golden
Globe® and Tony® winning songwriters. It is a joyous, provocative,
and hilarious evening for everyone who is 50, knows anyone who is
50 or plans to be 50.

"A classy music-and-comedy celebration! It will make a lot of
people feel empowered. It does so with integrity, craft, and heart!"
– *Chicago Tribune*

Hats! is inspired by the experiences, philosophies, and mission of
the Red Hat Society.

OTHER TITLES AVAILABLE FROM SAMUEL FRENCH

...AND BABY MAKES TWO

Nanci Christopher

Dramartic Comedy / 1f

A single woman's desire to experience motherhood without a husband at her side sends her through the world of adoption. Her path leads her through an array of characters and situations rife with drama. Settling on private adoption through an attorney she suffers an unfathomable heartbreak at the death of her newborn son. She is somehow able to rise out of despair to try again and meets Elizabeth who is looking for someone to adopt her unborn child. A new family is forged through the courage of two very brave women. The running time is one hour.

...And Baby Makes Two – an adoption tale was nominated for the 2009 **SUSAN SMITH BLACKBURN PRIZE**

"Christopher's messages about love and following your dreams are worth telling...fascinating material."
– *Backstage West*

OTHER TITLES AVAILABLE FROM SAMUEL FRENCH

THE MAKEOVER

Patsy Hester Daussat

Dramatic Comedy / 4m, 4f, 1m or f / Interior Set

It's a typical Saturday evening, as Mike and Melanie play games with their best friends, Victor and Paula. They have been neighbors for years, and each have a son home from college for the summer. Little does Melanie know that her happy, comfortable world will soon be thrown into turmoil. Mike has sent a letter to Facing Facts, Melanie and Paula's favorite reality television show. He believes Melanie, who has gained weight over the years, would be thrilled to have a make-over at Facing Facts' fabulous spa. After all, she and Paula rave about it. Unfortunately, every Monday night when Melanie and Paula watch the show, their husbands leave to play baseball. Poor Mike is clueless about the show's cruel, ratings-hungry hostess, Frances Montgomery, who thrives on humiliating those who are ambushed on the show. When the Facing Facts crew descends at her door, Melanie endures a disastrous ambush. Afterward, she cannot understand why Mike would subject her to national humiliation. Melanie tells him to be out of the house when she returns from the spa. Mike is hopeful that she will change her mind, but things only get worse the evening Melanie returns. Frances not only belittles Melanie again, she sets her sights on an oblivious Mike. Melanie finally explodes, throwing the Facing Facts crew out of her house, along with Mike. Events in the days that follow bring Melanie to realizations about herself and the important things in life.

"Daussat knows the basics of writing a situational script: She sets up the characters and action nicely, and gives the characters interesting quirks and vibrant lines to speak…(The) message about learning to love yourself (is) peppered with…comedy (and is) heartfelt…*The Makeover* should become a popular title in theaters…"
– *Fort Worth Star Telegram*

OTHER TITLES AVAILABLE FROM SAMUEL FRENCH

SECRETS OF A SOCCER MOM

Kathleen Clark

Comedy / 3f / Exterior

Three engaging women reluctantly take the field in a mothers vs. sons soccer game. They intend to let the children win, but as the game unfolds they become intent on scoring. The competition ignites a fierce desire to recapture their youthful good-humor, independence and sexiness, paving the way toward a better understanding of themselves, their families and changes they need to make in their lives.

"Let's hear it for *Soccer Moms,* a diverting comedy with a slick style and attention, holding crisp dialogue."
– *The New York Times*

"A sympathetic and compelling comedy with constant laughs."
– *Variety*

"Soccer moms of the world, unite and jog over to enjoy Kathleen Clark's new comedy."
– *Associated Press*

"*Secrets of A Soccer Mom* puts the heart and 'sole' into comedy."
– *New York Daily News*

Breinigsville, PA USA
12 December 2010
251186BV00005B/6/P